PINOCCHIO

ILLUSTRATOR'S NOTE

Sitting in the darkened theatre next to my mother, I waited anxiously for the film to begin. Minutes into Walt Disney's "Pinocchio", I was lost in the magic and mystery of not only a puppet brought to life, but also in the creation of an entire imaginary world. "Pinocchio" was the first film I ever saw. It had a lasting impact on me. Its images are powerful and majestic, and it determined the course of my artistic career.

I love illustrating the classics, because they continue to inspire people today, as they always have throughout the years. Being able to paint the characters of classic literature as I see them has been a lifelong goal of mine. However, each time I illustrate a classic, I'm concerned because people who know the stories also have their own images of what the characters should look like. The story of Pinocchio left a deep impression on me, and I have always wanted to illustrate it. When we found this early translation of Collodi's original story, it gave me the ability and freedom to create new images based on Collodi's original words.

Going straight to the origins of the folktale, I placed the setting of this book in Italy. The environment of Italy provided me with bright and sunny lighting. There was a challenge in designing the puppet so that the wooden boy would be an appealing character. To paint him so that people could relate to him, I made a puppet to pose and combined him with a real boy. This helped me to give Pinocchio a human dimension. It is my pleasure to present to you the environments and characters, as I see them, in this edition of Pinocchio. I hope that you enjoy this book as much as I've enjoyed illustrating it.

PINOCCHIO

Illustrated by
GREG HILDEBRANDT
Story by CARLO COLLODI

The Unicorn Publishing House
New Jersey

Designed by Jean L. Scrocco
Edited by Heidi K. L. Corso and Karen Sardinas-Wyssling
Printed in Singapore by Singapore National Printers Ltd.
through Palace Press, San Francisco, CA
Reproduction Photography by the Color Wheel, New York, NY

♦ ♦ ♦ ♦ ♦

♦ ♦ ♦ ♦ ♦

Distributed in Canada by Doubleday Canada, Ltd., Toronto, ON

♦ ♦ ♦ ♦ ♦

Printing History 15 14 13 12 11 10 9 8 7 6 5 4 3 2

♦ ♦ ♦ ♦ ♦

Library of Congress Cataloging-in-Publication Data
Main entry under title:
Collodi, Carlo, 1826-1890
Pinocchio

Translation of: Avventure di Pinocchio
Summary: Pinocchio, a wooden puppet full of tricks and
mischief, with a talent for getting into and out of
trouble, wants more than anything else
to become a real boy.
(1. Puppets – Fiction. 2. Fairy Tales) I Hildebrandt,
Greg, ill. II. Title
PZ8.C7Ph 1988 (Fic) 87-80183
ISBN 0-88101-078-2

More Colorful Classics
In This
Easy-to-Read
Little Unicorn Classic Series

PETER PAN
ANTIQUE FAIRY TALES
THE WIZARD OF OZ
HEIDI
A CHRISTMAS CAROL
POLLYANNA
DAVY AND THE GOBLIN
TWENTY THOUSAND LEAGUES

CAST OF CHARACTERS

Paul Giacobbe • Pinocchio
Greg Hildebrandt • Geppetto
Krista Wetherill • Blue Fairy
Dan Conover • Master Cherry
William McGuire • Hawker of Old Clothes
Joseph D. Scrocco Sr. • Fire Eater
Michael Paglia • Coachman
Gene O'Brien • Director of Buffoons
Josephine Paglia • Village Lady
Mamie Scanzera • Village Lady
Norfie Osroc • Green Fisherman
Stephanie Pastuch • Miss Rose
Raphael Ramone • Harlequin
Robbie McCann • School Boy
Brian McGee • School Boy
Ollie Orriss • School Boy
Michael Donnelly • School Boy

LIST OF ILLUSTRATIONS

PINOCCHIO

There was once upon a time a piece of wood lying in the shop of an old carpenter called Master Cherry. It was only a common log like the ones that are burned in stoves and fireplaces. But Master Cherry beamed with delight at the wood. "This little piece of wood will do just right to make the leg of a table," he said.

Taking an ax, he struck the wood with a hard blow and heard a little voice cry, "Do not strike me so hard!" Imagine Master Cherry's fright! He looked all around the room to find out where the voice had come from. He looked under the bench and out the door, but saw nobody.

So he began to sand and polish the wood. While he was running the sand block up and down the wood, he heard the same little voice laugh, "Stop! You are tickling me all over!" This time poor Master Cherry fell down as if he had been struck by lightning.

At that moment someone knocked at the door. "Come in," said the carpenter, without having the strength to rise to his feet. In walked a jolly little old man with a wig as yellow as corn pudding. His name was Geppetto, but when the boys of the neighborhood wished to make him very angry, they called him by the nickname "Polendina," which means "yellow corn pudding."

"Good day," said Geppetto.

"What has brought you to me, friend Geppetto?"

"I thought I would make a beautiful wooden puppet, one that should know how to dance."

Master Cherry was pleased. He went right away to the bench and brought the piece of wood that had caused him so much fear. But just as he was going to give it to his friend, the piece of wood shook itself and struck poor Geppetto on the leg.

"Bravo, Polendina!" cried the little voice.

Geppetto became red from rage and turned to Master Cherry. "Is that the polite way you make a present — by insulting me?" Geppetto demanded.

"I swear to you, it was not I," said Master Cherry. The two went from words to blows — biting and fighting and scratching.

When the battle was over, Master Cherry had two scratches on his nose, and Geppetto's wig was in Master Cherry's teeth. Now that it was settled, they shook hands and swore to remain good friends for the rest of their lives. "Let us be friends as we were," said Geppetto. Geppetto thanked Master Cherry, then he carried off his fine piece of wood and returned limping to his house.

The Magic Wood Speaks

Geppetto lived in a small room. It had light only from a staircase. The furniture included a bad chair, a poor bed, and a broken-down table. As soon as he reached home, Geppetto set to work carving his puppet. "I shall call him Pinocchio," said Geppetto. He started by carving the head. When the eyes were finished, they looked around and then stared right at Geppetto. "Wicked wooden eyes," said Geppetto. "Why do you stare at me?"

No one answered.

He then started to carve the nose, but no sooner had he finished it, than it began to grow. It grew and grew and grew. Poor Geppetto tired himself out cutting it off, for the more he cut it, the longer it became.

The mouth was not even finished when it began to laugh at him. "Stop laughing!" roared an angry Geppetto. The mouth then stopped laughing, but put out its tongue as far as it would go. Geppetto pretended not to notice. He went on to make the chin, then the throat, then the shoulders, the stomach, the arms, and the hands.

The hands were scarcely finished when Geppetto felt his wig snatched from his head. He turned round and saw his yellow wig in the puppet's hand. He demanded it back, but instead of returning it, Pinocchio put it on his own head. At this rude behavior, Geppetto felt sadder than he had ever been in his life before. He turned to Pinocchio and said to him, "You young rascal! You are already showing a lack of respect to your father. That is bad, my boy, very bad!" Geppetto dried a tear. The legs and the feet needed to be done.

When Geppetto had finished the feet, Pinocchio kicked him. "I deserve it!" he said to himself.

Geppetto Carves Pinocchio

He took the puppet under the arms and placed him on the floor to teach him to walk. Pinocchio's legs were stiff and he could not move. Geppetto led him by the hand and showed him how to put one foot before the other. When his legs were no longer stiff, Pinocchio began to walk by himself and to run about the room. Suddenly, he jumped through the door, into the street and ran away.

Poor Geppetto rushed after him, but was not able to stop him. That rascal Pinocchio leaped in front of him like a rabbit. "Stop him! Stop him!" shouted Geppetto. But the people in the street, seeing a wooden puppet running like a racehorse, stood still in wonder and laughed and laughed and laughed.

At last, a soldier came. Hearing the noise, he imagined that a horse had escaped from its master. He planted his legs in the middle of the road and caught Pinocchio cleverly by his large nose. The soldier handed Pinocchio over to Geppetto, who would have pulled the puppet's ears, but there were none. He had forgotten to make them.

Pinocchio threw himself on the ground and began to weep. The crowd of people gathered around the puppet. "Poor puppet! Geppetto seems a good man, but with boys he's mean! If that poor puppet is left in his hands, who knows how Geppetto will beat him!" they said. It ended that the soldier at last set Pinocchio free and took poor Geppetto to jail.

Well then, children, I must tell you that while poor Geppetto was being taken to jail for no fault of his own, Pinocchio ran home to Geppetto's house. He found the door open. As he came in, he heard someone saying, "Cri-cri-cri!"

Pinocchio Runs Away

"Who calls me?" said Pinocchio in a fright.

"It is I!"

Pinocchio turned and saw a big cricket crawling slowly up the wall.

"I am the Talking Cricket," said the insect. "I have lived in this room for a hundred years."

"This room is mine now," said the puppet. "If you would do me a favor, go away at once."

"I will not go until I have told you a great truth. Woe to those boys who are bad to their parents. They will never come to any good in this world and will pay bitterly," replied the Cricket.

"Sing away, Cricket," said Pinocchio. "I am running away tomorrow because I will not go to school like other boys. I have no wish to learn. I want to eat, drink, sleep, and have fun."

"Poor little goose!" said the Cricket. "Don't you know that you will grow up to be a donkey?"

"Hold your tongue, you mean insect!" shouted Pinocchio.

"Poor Pinocchio. As a wooden puppet, you will have a wooden head," said the Cricket. At these words an angry Pinocchio snatched up a wooden hammer. He threw it at the Cricket. Perhaps he never meant to hit him, but sadly it killed him.

Night was coming on, and Pinocchio had eaten nothing all day. He began to feel hungry. He ran about the room searching everywhere in hopes of finding a crust, a bone left by a dog, or a little moldy pudding. But he could find nothing, nothing at all.

Pinocchio Kills the Talking Cricket

It was a stormy night. The thunder was loud and the sky seemed on fire with lightning. But Pinocchio's hunger was stronger than his fear, so he ran through the rain to the village, hoping to beg a little bread. There was nobody about, however, and Pinocchio had to return home not only hungry, but tired and wet. He sat down and rested his wet feet on a pan full of burning coals and fell asleep. While he slept his wooden feet took fire and slowly burned to ashes.

When he heard knocking at the door the next morning, he got up and fell trying to answer it. He couldn't walk. The knocking was Geppetto.

"Let me in, you rascal," shouted Geppetto from the street.

"Dear Papa, I cannot!" cried the puppet, rolling about on the ground.

"Open the door, I tell you!" repeated Geppetto.

Geppetto climbed up the wall and got in at the window. When he found Pinocchio had no feet, he took him in his arms and kissed him. Pinocchio told his father what had happened and said he was starving. Geppetto took the puppet in his arms again. He gave him three pears from his pocket, which were for his own breakfast. Pinocchio quickly ate the pears and then began to grumble that he wanted new feet.

Geppetto made a new pair of feet for the puppet after Pinocchio promised to go to school. As he was very poor, Geppetto made Pinocchio a suit out of paper, a pair of shoes from tree bark, and a cap of a crumb of bread.

"But Papa," said Pinocchio, "I still need a spelling book."

Geppetto Rescues Pinocchio

Geppetto put on his old worn coat and ran out of the house. He returned shortly, in his shirt sleeves, holding in his hand a spelling book for Pinocchio. The old coat was gone. The poor man was in his shirt sleeves in the cold because he had sold his coat to buy Pinocchio's spelling book. Pinocchio threw his arms round Geppetto and kissed him.

The next day Pinocchio set out for school with his spelling book under his arm. As he went along, he began to dream aloud, "Today at school I will learn to read, tomorrow I will begin to write, and the day after tomorrow I will learn math. Then I will earn a great deal of money to buy Papa a beautiful new coat with diamond buttons."

Yet, as he walked, he heard the sound of pipes and drums. He stopped and listened. Should he go to school or follow the pipes? He stood still for a moment. Then Pinocchio decided to follow the pipes that day and go to school the next. The merry sounds led to a tent with a puppet show inside. Pinocchio longed to see the show and sold his new spelling book to a seller with old clothes for the price of a ticket. And to think that poor Geppetto was at home shaking with cold in his shirt sleeves just so he might buy Pinocchio a book!

When Pinocchio entered the little puppet theater, Harlequin and Punchinello were on stage. As usual they were fighting and planning every moment to come to blows. The audience laughed and laughed as they listened to these two puppets.

Harlequin suddenly stopped short and excitedly pointed and called out, "It is Pinocchio! It is our brother, Pinocchio! Long live Pinocchio!" The other puppets

Pinocchio Sells His Spelling Book

reached out to him with joy and Pinocchio made a leap onto the stage.

How long the party of hugs and friendly pinches would have gone on I do not know, for at that moment, out came the showman, Fire Eater. He was very big and so ugly that the sight of him was enough to frighten anyone. Fire Eater was angry that his show was being delayed. All of the puppets shook.

"Take that puppet backstage!" he roared. "Tonight we will settle the payment!"

As soon as the play was over, Fire Eater ordered Pinocchio to be used for firewood. Pinocchio was dragged forward screaming, "Papa, Papa, save me! I will not die! I will not die!"

Fire Eater, who really had a soft heart, felt sorry for Pinocchio. He listened to Pinocchio's story. As was his habit when very moved, he began to sneeze. He asked Pinocchio about his father. When he found out that the puppet's father was poor, he handed Pinocchio five gold pieces. "Give them to your father from me."

Pinocchio joyfully thanked the showman, and started home. He had not gone far when he met a Fox who was lame in one foot, and a Cat blind in both eyes. The Fox walked leaning on the Cat, who in turn, was led down the road by the Fox.

"Good day, Pinocchio," said the Fox.

"Good day," said Pinocchio. "How do you know my name?"

"I know your father well," said the Fox. "I saw him yesterday at the door of his house, shivering in his shirt sleeves with cold."

Fire Eater the Tyrant

"Poor Papa! But that is over now; for in the future he shall shiver no more! I have five gold pieces." And Pinocchio pulled out the money that Fire Eater had given to him.

At the sound of the money, the Fox stretched out the paw that had seemed crippled, and the Cat opened wide two eyes that looked like green lanterns. It is true that she shut them again and so quickly that Pinocchio noticed nothing.

"How would you like to make a thousand gold pieces out of your miserable five?" asked the Fox suddenly.

"I should think so!" said Pinocchio, "but how?"

"Come with us," said the Fox. "There is a field. It is called the Field of Miracles. In this field you must dig a little hole and you must bury your money. In the morning, when you get up and return to the field you will find a beautiful tree loaded with gold."

Pinocchio was so happy that he forgot all about Geppetto and said to the Fox and the Cat, "Let us be off at once. I will go with you."

They walked and walked until at last, toward evening, they arrived very tired at the Inn of the Red Crawfish. "Let us stop here a little," said the Fox, "to get something to eat and to rest ourselves for an hour or two. We will start again at midnight." When they had gone into the inn, they sat down to dinner, but none of them was very hungry.

The Cat, who had a stomachache and was feeling very tired, could eat only thirty-five fishes with tomato sauce, and four portions of noodles with butter and cheese. The Fox, whose doctor had put him on a very strict diet, was forced to content himself simply with a rabbit with fat chickens and early hens. After the rabbit, he had a dish of

The Five Gold Pieces

partridges, frogs, lizards, and other goodies. The one who ate the least was Pinocchio. He asked for some walnuts and a little bread, and left everything on his plate.

After dinner he fell asleep. The innkeeper woke him at midnight. "Your friends left two hours ago without you and will meet you at the Field of Miracles tomorrow morning at daybreak," the innkeeper explained.

Pinocchio traveled all night on a dark road until he saw a tiny glowing light on the trunk of a tree. "I am the ghost of the Talking Cricket," said the insect in a low voice. "I want to give you some advice. Go back to your poor father who is weeping because you have never returned to him. Don't trust those who promise to make you rich in a day. The night is dark and full of murderers."

"Really," said Pinocchio to himself, "That Cricket thinks I am to meet with murderers! That is of little matter, for I don't believe in murderers. I have never believed in them. For me, I think that murderers have been made up by papas to frighten boys who want to go out at night."

But Pinocchio had not time to finish his thinking, for at that moment two evil-looking figures covered in charcoal sacks were running after him. Not knowing where to hide his gold pieces, he put them in his mouth under his tongue.

Then he tried to escape. But he had not gone a step when he felt himself grabbed by the arm and heard two horrid voices saying to him:

"Your money or your life!"

Pinocchio was unable to talk because of the money in his mouth. He made a thousand signs that he was only a poor puppet who had no money.

At The Red Crawfish

"Come now! Out with the money!" The murderers shook him. Pinocchio shook his head as if he had no money.

"Give us your money or you are dead!" cried the tallest murderer. "And after you are dead we will kill your father!"

"Oh no! Not my poor Papa!" cried Pinocchio. But as he said it, the coins clinked in his mouth.

"Ah!" cried the murderers. "The money is in your mouth! Give it to us at once!" One of the murderers took a knife and tried to force it between Pinocchio's lips. As quick as lightning, Pinocchio caught the hand with his teeth. In one bite he bit it clean off and spit it out. He was surprised to see that it was a cat's paw.

He got away from the murderers and began to run. After he had raced some miles, he could run no more. Then he climbed the trunk of a very high pine tree in the wood and sat in the top-most branches. The murderers tried to climb after him, but halfway up the trunk they slid down. Collecting a quantity of dry wood, they piled it beneath the pine and set it on fire. The pine began to burn and to flame like a candle in the wind. Pinocchio saw that the flames were getting higher every instant. He made a huge leap from the top of the tree and started afresh across the fields and yards. At first he thought that the murderers had given up. Looking back he saw that they were both running after him, still covered in their sacks.

At this sight the puppet started to give up. Turning his eyes in every direction, however, he saw far away a small house as white as snow. "If only I can reach that house," he thought, "perhaps I should be saved." He ran for his life

Pinocchio Flees the Assassins

for nearly two hours. At last he arrived at the door of the house and knocked.

No one answered. He knocked again very, very hard, for he heard the sound of steps coming toward him, and the heavy panting of the murderers.

Seeing that knocking was useless, he began to kick the door with all his might. The window then opened and a beautiful Child appeared at it. She had blue hair and a face as white as a waxen image; her eyes were closed and her hands were crossed on her breast. "In this house," she said in a voice that seemed to come from the other world, "there is no one who can help you. We are all dead." Having said this, she disappeared, and the window was closed again without any noise.

Suddenly, Pinocchio felt himself grabbed by the collar, and the same two horrible voices said to him, "You shall not escape from us again. Let us hang him!" They tied his arms behind him, passed a rope around his neck and then hanged him to the branch of a tree called the Big Oak. "Good-bye till tomorrow. Let us hope that when we return you will be polite enough to allow yourself to be found quite dead. Then we shall take the gold from your opened mouth." And they walked off.

Little by little, Pinocchio's eyes began to grow dim. Although he felt that death was near, he continued to hope that some kind person would come to help him before it was too late. He stammered out, "Oh Papa! Papa! If only you were here!" His breath failed him and he could say no more. He shut his eyes, opened his mouth and gave a long shudder.

The Magical Haven

While poor Pinocchio was hanging from the branch of the Big Oak, the beautiful Child with blue hair came to the window. Feeling sorry for him, she had Pinocchio carried into her home.

Now I must tell you that the Child with the blue hair was no more and no less than a beautiful Fairy. For more than a thousand years she had lived in the wood!

The Fairy sent for the most famous doctors in the neighborhood: a Crow, an Owl, and a Talking Cricket. They came right away. The Crow declared the puppet dead; the Owl declared the puppet alive. The Talking Cricket said, "I believe that when a doctor does not know what he is talking about, he should remain silent. However, I know this puppet." Pinocchio started to shake. "He is a do-nothing, a wanderer, and a bad son who will make his poor father die of a broken heart."

Pinocchio hid under the sheets and sobbed. "When a dead person cries, it is a sign that he is on the road to get well," said the Crow.

"I disagree," said the Owl. "I believe that when a dead person cries, it is a sign that he is sorry to die." The three doctors left the room.

The Fairy saw that Pinocchio had a very high fever. She took out some medicine. "Drink this," she said. "It will cure you."

Pinocchio looked at this medicine, and said, "Is it sweet or bitter? If it is bitter I will not drink it!" said Pinocchio.

"You will die," the Fairy warned.

"I do not care! I will not drink it!" cried Pinocchio.

The Blue Fairy Calls The Doctors

The Fairy clapped her hands. Immediately two black rabbits who were grave diggers appeared and began to measure Pinocchio for a grave. "Oh," cried Pinocchio. "Give me the medicine. I will drink it!" He quickly drank the medicine. In a few moments, he was as well as ever.

The Fairy smiled at Pinocchio and asked him for his story. As Pinocchio told her, she asked, "And the gold pieces, where have you put them?"

"I have lost them!" said Pinocchio. He was telling a lie, for he had them in his pocket. He had scarcely told the lie when his nose began to grow. At once it was two fingers longer.

"And where did you lose them?"

"I lost them in the wood near here," continued Pinocchio, growing confused. At this second lie, his nose went on growing.

"If you have lost them in the wood near here, we will look for them, and we shall find them," said the Fairy, "because everything that is lost in that wood is always found."

"Ah! Now I remember," said Pinocchio, getting mixed up. "I didn't lose the gold pieces. I swallowed them by accident!" At this third lie, his nose grew so long that poor Pinocchio could not move in any direction.

"What lies you have told," laughed the Fairy. "There are two kinds of lies, Pinocchio: lies that have long noses and lies that have short legs. Your lie is one of those that has a long nose."

Pinocchio didn't know where to hide himself from shame. The Fairy, however, let the puppet cry for a good half hour over his nose to teach him a lesson. She wanted to correct his awful habit of telling lies. Then she clapped

Pinocchio Tells A Lie

her hands together. A thousand woodpeckers came and pecked Pinocchio's nose down to the right normal size.

"Stay here and be my little brother and I shall be your good little sister," said the Fairy. "I have already let your father know, and he will be coming here tonight. Go and meet him. Take the road through the wood." Pinocchio happily set out. As soon as he was in the wood he began to run like a deer. But when he got to a certain spot, almost in front of the Big Oak, he met the Fox and the Cat.

"Why here is our dear Pinocchio!" cried the Fox, kissing him. "Come with us to the Field of Miracles! Bury your money there and go home with your pockets full." Pinocchio was surprised to see that the cat had somehow lost a paw. He foolishly decided to go with them and followed them to the Field. There, he buried his money, and promised the Fox and the Cat beautiful presents.

"We wish for no presents," answered the two rascals. "It is enough for us to have taught you the way to make money without doing hard work." Pinocchio joyfully went back to town alone. After dinner, he went back to the Field. When he saw no money tree, he knew that the Fox and the Cat had robbed him. Angrily, he rushed back to town to see the judge, who was a gorilla. He accused the two tricksters who had robbed him.

The judge listened and was unhappy for him. When the puppet had no more to say, the judge called to his guards. "This poor devil has been robbed. Put him into jail, right away." Pinocchio was frightened to hear this sentence, but the guards quickly carried him off to jail.

Pinocchio was in jail for four months. When he was set free, he took the road that led to the Fairy's house. Soon

The Gorilla Judge

he reached the field where the little white house had once stood. But the little white house was no longer there. He saw instead a marble stone, which had engraved on it these sad words:

HERE LIES THE CHILD
WITH THE BLUE HAIR
WHO DIED FROM SORROW
AFTER SHE WAS ABANDONED
BY HER LITTLE BROTHER, PINOCCHIO

I leave you to imagine Pinocchio's feelings when he read the stone. He fell with his face on the ground. Covering the tombstone with a thousand kisses, he burst into a flood of tears. He cried all night, and when morning came he was still crying. As he wept he said, "Oh, little Fairy, why did you die?"

Just then, a large bird flew over his head. Stopping, it called down to him, "Do you happen to know a puppet who is called Pinocchio?"

"Pinocchio? I am Pinocchio!" cried the puppet, jumping to his feet.

"Your father is looking for you," cried the bird. "I saw him three days ago on the seashore. He was building a little boat for himself, to cross the oceans until he finds you. If you wish, I will carry you to him."

Without waiting for more, Pinocchio jumped at once on the back of the bird.

The bird flew away. Soon they were so high that they almost touched the clouds. They flew all night and the next morning they reached the seashore.

Pinocchio's Heart Breaks

When Pinocchio arrived, the shore was crowded with people who were looking out to sea. An old woman told Pinocchio, "A poor father who has lost his son has gone away in a boat to look for him on the other side of the water. Today the sea is rough and the little boat is in danger of sinking."

Looking out at the stormy sea, Pinocchio was frightened to see his father far away in a little boat on the angry waves. Pinocchio stood on a high rock, calling to his father and waving with his hands and cap. At last, he jumped into the sea crying, "I will save my papa!"

Pinocchio, being made of wood, floated easily and swam like a fish. He swam all night. And what an awful night it was! The rain came down hard. There was thunder and lightning and hail.

Toward morning, he saw an island. All of a sudden, he was washed upon the shore. He felt better and said, "This time I have made a wonderful escape from the wild sea!"

After walking for a half an hour he reached a village. A little woman came by carrying two cans of water. He helped to carry the cans to her house in exchange for a dish of cauliflower and a piece of bread. Once inside, Pinocchio looked at the woman with wonder. "Oh-h-h-h! It is ... you are like ... the same eyes ... the same hair ... Oh, little Fairy! Tell me it is you!" Throwing himself on the floor Pinocchio began to cry.

The little woman, realizing that Pinocchio recognized her, admitted that she was the Fairy, grown up. Pinocchio promised her that he would be good and go to school. The Fairy promised that she would be his mama and that some-day he could be a real boy.

The Blue Fairy in Disguise

"I will study, I will work, I will do all that you tell me, for I am tired of being a puppet, and I wish at any price to become a boy."

Pinocchio was true to his word. He was the first into school and the last to leave. Imagine the delight of all the little boys when they saw a puppet walk into their school! They set up a roar of laughter that never ended. They played tricks on the poor puppet. One boy carried off his cap, another pulled his jacket. One tried to give him ink on his face, another tried to tie strings to his feet and hands to make him dance. Unfortunately, he made friends with several young rascals who disliked school.

One day Pinocchio's friends said that the great Dogfish was at the shore. He skipped school with them to go and see. When he arrived at the shore, there was no Dogfish. The sea was as smooth as a lake. From his friends' silly laughter, Pinocchio understood that they had been making a fool of him. Angry words led to blows, and schoolbooks were thrown.

Suddenly, a giant crab came out of the water and in a rough voice said, "Take care, Pinocchio! The fights of boys never end well!" Pinocchio did not pay attention. The next moment, one of the boys, trying to hit Pinocchio, struck his friend, Eugene, instead. Eugene turned white as a sheet and fell on the sand.

Thinking he was dead, the frightened boys ran off as hard as their legs could carry them, and in a few minutes they were out of sight. But Pinocchio stayed, crying bitterly. He struck his head with his fists and called poor Eugene by his name. Suddenly, two soldiers came by and, not listening to Pinocchio's story, they carried him toward the

The Giant Crab Warns Pinocchio

village jail. When a gust of wind blew Pinocchio's cap off his head and carried it ten yards away, he was allowed to get it. The puppet went and picked up his cap. Instead of putting it on his head, he took it between his teeth and ran quickly as hard as he could toward the seashore.

The soldiers sent a guard dog, Alidoro, after him. In order to escape, Pinocchio jumped into the sea, but Alidoro fell in after him and began to drown. Pinocchio, who had a good heart, saved the dog. Then he swam away.

Suddenly, he found himself in a huge fish net, being drawn out of the sea. A strange green fisherman carried his net full of fish into his cave. He pulled out the fish one by one, enjoying his feast.

When the fisherman pulled Pinocchio from the net, he said, "A puppet? A puppet is quite a new fish for me. I shall enjoy eating this." The fisherman put flour on each fish, including Pinocchio. He threw the fish into hot oil. Pinocchio began to beg for his life. Just then his new friend, Alidoro, entered the cave. He had smelled the frying fish. Seeing Pinocchio's problem, Alidoro grabbed the puppet in his mouth and ran away. Pinocchio thanked Alidoro and walked back to the village. He wore no clothes and still had a light dusting of flour. Stopping by a cottage, Pinocchio first asked about Eugene. An old man said Eugene was alive and had returned home. Pinocchio was given an old flour sack. With a pair of scissors he cut a hole at the end and at each side, and put it on like a shirt. With this clothing he set off for the village.

When he reached the village, it was night and very dark. A storm had come on and the rain was coming down

Caught By the Green Fisherman

heavily. He went straight to the Fairy's house, knocked at the door, and hoped to be let in.

A window opened. The Fairy's maid, a big Snail with a lighted candle on her head, looked out a window. It was on the top floor of a four-story house. Pinocchio begged to be let inside.

"I will come down and open the door right away," said the Snail. When Pinocchio asked the Snail to hurry, she said, "My boy, I am a snail, and snails are never in a hurry."

The next morning at daybreak the door was at last opened. That clever little Snail had taken only nine hours to come down from the fourth story to the door. Pinocchio, either from hunger or from being tired, had fainted away.

When he woke up, the Fairy was beside him. "I will forgive you once more," she said, "but woe to you if you behave badly a third time."

Pinocchio promised to do his best. For the rest of the year, he was so good that the Fairy said to him, "Tomorrow you shall become a real boy!" Pinocchio joyfully set out to tell his friends the news and invite them to a party.

Now I must tell you that among Pinocchio's friends, and schoolfellows, there was one that he was very fond of. Candlewick was the most lazy and naughty boy in the school, but Pinocchio liked him very much. He found his best friend hiding under a porch. "I cannot come to the party," said Candlewick. "Tonight I am going to the Land of Boobies. The days there are spent in play and amusement from morning until night. Nobody ever studies! There are no schools! That is the country for me! What do you think of it? A coach will come for us soon. Will you not go with me? Yes or no?"

The Blue Fairy's Handmaiden

Pinocchio hesitated. "No, no, and again no," he said, "I promised the good Fairy to become a good boy, and I will keep my word. I must — " His words were stopped at the arrival of the coach. Drawn by twelve pairs of donkeys, the coach was full of boys.

The coachman turned to Pinocchio with a thousand smirks and said, "Tell me, my fine boy, what do you intend to do? Are you coming with us?"

Pinocchio sighed and finally said, "Make a little room for me. I am coming too." However, there was no room inside the coach. Pinocchio had to get on a donkey.

At daybreak they arrived at the Land of Boobies. It was a country unlike any other in the world. To sum it up, there was such merriment, such laughter, such an uproar that nowhere could there be more happy boys. There were constant games and amusements. Five months passed like lightning, with no thought of books or study. Then, one morning, Pinocchio woke up to a terrible surprise that put him in a very bad mood.

What was this surprise? I will tell you, my dear little readers. The surprise was that when Pinocchio awoke and scratched his head, he found ... Can you guess in the least what he found it was?

He found to his great surprise that his ears had grown so long that they seemed like two brooms. He went at once looking for a mirror so he might see himself. But he was not able to find one, so he filled the bowl of his washing stand with water. He looked in there and saw he had a lovely pair of donkey ears!

Imagine his sorrow and shame! He began to cry and roar. He beat his head against the wall. But the more he

To the Land of the Boobies

cried, the longer his ears grew. They grew and grew, and became hairy toward the points. At the sound of his loud cries, a beautiful little Woodchuck that lived on the first floor came into the room. "I am ill," wept Pinocchio.

"My friend," the Woodchuck said sighing, "I am sorry to tell you some bad news. You have a very bad fever called donkey fever. In two hours you shall become a little donkey, for boys who are lazy and dislike school and books end up becoming donkeys."

Pinocchio set out to look for Candlewick. He found him at his house, with donkey ears on his head. When Pinocchio and Candlewick saw each other, they began to laugh. But while they were laughing, Candlewick suddenly stopped, staggered, and changed right into a donkey. Then Pinocchio too, turned into a little grey donkey and began to bray loudly, "J-a, j-a, j-a."

While this was going on, someone knocked at the door, and a voice on the outside said, "Open the door! I am the coachman, who brought you here. Open at once or it will be the worse for you!" When the two donkeys could not open the door, the little man opened it with a hard kick. Coming into the room, he said to Pinocchio and Candlewick with a little laugh, "Well done, boys! You brayed well and I knew you by your voices. That is why I am here."

At these words the two little donkeys were stunned. They stood with their heads down, their ears down low, and their tails between their legs. At first the little man stroked them gently. Then he combed them roughly until they shone like two mirrors. Then he put a halter round their necks and led them to the market place, in hopes of selling them and making a lot of money.

The Fate of Bad Boys

And now, my little readers, you will understand how this little man worked. The wicked little monster, who had a face all milk and honey, often made trips round the world with his coach. As he went along, he collected, with promises and praise, all the lazy boys who hated school and did not care to study. Then, when his coach was full, he would take them to the Land of Boobies. There they might pass their time in games, in laughter, and in amusement. When these poor, tricked boys, from playing all the time and no study, had become so many little donkeys, he took hold of them with great delight and carried them off to the fairs and markets to be sold. In this way he had in a few years made heaps of money and had become very, very rich.

What became of Candlewick I do not know, but I do know that Pinocchio, from the very first day, had to live a hard life. He was sold to a circus. Pinocchio was put into a stall. His master filled the stall with straw for him to eat. Pinocchio tried a mouthful and spat it out. The master then filled the stall with hay. Pinocchio tried another mouthful and spat it out too. Then the master got angry. He whipped Pinocchio.

"Do you mean that a little Donkey like you has to be fed chicken and cake? I bought you to make money for me!" He slammed the door of the stall.

Pinocchio was hungry. He tried the hay. It wasn't very good, but it was filling. "How much better it would have been if I had gone to school!"

He was taught to jump through hoops, dance nicely, and stand up on his front legs. He got only straw and hay

Pinocchio is Sold at the Market

to eat, and often he got whippings that nearly took off his skin.

At last, the day came that Pinocchio performed for a crowd. He was dressed for the show, with a new bridle and ribbons and two white flowers in his ears. His mane was divided and curled. He was, in fact, a little donkey to fall in love with!

As he danced, amid a burst of shouts and clapping of hands, he raised his head and looked up. In the crowd was a beautiful lady who wore round her neck a thick, gold chain from which hung a medal. On the medal was painted a picture of a puppet. "That is my picture! That lady is the Fairy!" said Pinocchio to himself. Overcome with joy he tried to cry out, "Oh, my little Fairy!"

But instead of these words, a bray came from his throat. The audience laughed. His master punished him with a hard rap on the nose to give him a lesson, and to make him understand that it is not good manners to bray before the audience. When the poor little donkey opened his eyes and looked up a second time, he saw that the Fairy was gone. His eyes filled with tears.

Sadly, while jumping through a hoop that night, Pinocchio caught his right leg and fell on the ground. When he got up, he was lame. It was with great difficulty that he managed to return to the stable.

The next morning the doctor of animals said that the donkey would remain lame for life. Since the circus had no use for a lame donkey, he was sold to a man wanting to make a drum from his skin. Imagine poor Pinocchio's feelings when he heard that he was going to be a drum!

The Donkey on Display

He was taken to the seashore, a stone put round his neck and a rope tied round his leg. Then he was thrown into the water to drown. Pinocchio, weighed down by the stone, went at once to the bottom. The man who bought him kept tight hold of the rope. He sat down on a rock to wait until the donkey drowned.

When the man pulled Pinocchio up by the rope fifty minutes later, he found a live puppet instead of a dead donkey. A large school of fish had eaten away all of the donkey, leaving the hard wood underneath. Pinocchio ran away from the man, jumped into the water and swam away.

While he was swimming, he saw the horrible head of a sea monster rising out of the water. This monster was no more and no less than that huge Dogfish. Think of poor Pinocchio's terror at the sight of the monster. He tried to avoid it, to change his direction, but the monster overtook him. Drawing in his breath, the Dogfish sucked in the poor puppet as he would have sucked in a hen's egg and swallowed him.

Inside the Dogfish, all was dark. Pinocchio sat in terror next to a poor Tunny who was swallowed by the Dogfish at the same time Pinocchio was. As the two sat, Pinocchio noticed a light in the distance. He decided to follow it and see what was there.

Pinocchio slowly began to move in the dark, through the body of the Dogfish. He took a step at a time in the direction of the light. The light became brighter as Pinocchio came closer. He walked and walked until at last he reached it, and when he reached it ... what did he find? I shall give you a thousand guesses.

Swallowed By The Dog Fish

He found a little table spread out with a lighted candle stuck into a green glass bottle. Seated at the table was a little old man. He was eating some live fish, and they were so very much alive that while he was eating them, they sometimes, even jumped out of his mouth.

At this sight, Pinocchio was filled with such great joy. He wanted to laugh; he wanted to cry; he wanted to say a thousand things. Instead he could only utter a cry of joy, open his arms, throw them round the little old man's neck, and shout out, "Oh, my dear Papa! I have found you at last! I will never leave you!"

"Then my eyes tell me true?" said Geppetto. "You are really my dear Pinocchio?"

"Yes, yes, I am Pinocchio, really Pinocchio! And you have forgiven me, have you not?"

Pinocchio poured out his story in a confused manner. Geppetto told him how he had managed to survive two years, using the things from a ship that the Dogfish had swallowed. "But now," finished Geppetto, "I have arrived at the end. There is nothing left and this candle that you see burning is the last that remains."

"Then, dear little Papa," said Pinocchio, "there is no time to lose. We must think of escaping."

Without another word Pinocchio took the candle in his hand and, going in front to light the way, he said to his father: "Follow me, and do not be afraid."

Pinocchio and Geppetto walked for some time and crossed the body and the stomach of the Dogfish. When they arrived at the point where the monster's big throat began, they thought it better to stop to give a good look round and to choose the best moment for escaping.

Pinocchio and Geppetto Reunited

Now I must tell you that the Dogfish was very old. He had trouble with his breathing and had a bad heart. Because of this, he had to sleep with his mouth open. When they got to the entrance to the throat, Pinocchio and his father looked up and could see beyond the huge open mouth a large piece of starry sky and beautiful moonlight. "This is the moment to escape: the Dogfish is sleeping. The sea is calm, and it is as light as day," whispered Pinocchio. "We will throw ourselves in the sea and swim away."

"I don't know how to swim," replied Geppetto.

"I am a good swimmer, Papa. You can get on my shoulders and I shall carry you safely to shore." As soon as Geppetto climbed onto Pinocchio's shoulders, Pinocchio, feeling sure of himself, threw himself into the water and began to swim. The sea was smooth and Pinocchio traveled quickly. Soon, he found that his Papa was shivering. Was it from fear or from the cold? Pinocchio thought that Geppetto was afraid. "Courage, Papa." he said. "In a few minutes we shall be safely on shore."

"But where is this shore?" asked Geppetto. "I can see nothing but the sea."

"But I am like a cat. I can see better by night."

Poor Pinocchio was only trying to keep his father's spirits up. But his strength began to fail him. Although he tried to seem like he was in good spirits, in reality he was beginning to feel bad. At last, he could do no more, and the shore was still far off.

Pinocchio swam until he had no breath left. Then he turned his head to Geppetto and said in broken words:

"Papa ... help me ... I am dying!"

The Escape

The father and son were on the point of drowning when they heard a voice asking, "Who is it that is dying?"

Pinocchio saw that it was Tunny, who had sat in the Dogfish's mouth with Pinocchio. He offered to give them a ride. "You must take hold of my tail and allow me to guide you. I will take you to shore."

Geppetto and Pinocchio, I need not tell you, accepted the offer at once. But instead of holding on by his tail, they thought it would be more comfortable to get on Tunny's back. "How did you manage to escape, dear Tunny?" asked Pinocchio.

"I followed you," said the Tunny. "You showed me the road, and I escaped after you."

"Tunny, you came at the right moment. You have saved my papa's life. I can find no words to thank you."

When they reached the shore, Pinocchio sprang onto land first so that he might help his father do the same. Then he turned to the Tunny and said to him in a voice full of love, "Permit me to give you a kiss as a sign of my endless thanks." The Tunny put his head out of the water, and Pinocchio, kneeling on the ground, kissed him softly on the mouth. At this proof of love, the poor Tunny, who was not used to it, was very touched. Not wanting to let himself be seen crying like a child, he plunged under the water and disappeared.

By this time, the day had dawned. Pinocchio, offering his arm to Geppetto, who had hardly any breath to stand, said to him:

"Lean on my arm, dear Papa, and let us go. We shall walk very slowly like the ants, and when we are tired we can rest by the wayside."

Rescued By the Tunny

"And where shall we go?" asked Geppetto.

"We shall look for some house or cottage where they will give us a little bread, and a little straw to serve as a bed."

They had not gone a hundred yards when they saw, begging by the roadside, two mean-looking people.

They were the Fox and the Cat, but it was hard to identify them. Fancy! The Cat had so long pretended to be blind that she had become blind in reality. The Fox, old, mangy, and unable to move one side of his body, did not even have his tail left. That sneaking thief, having fallen into trouble, had sold his beautiful tail.

"Oh Pinocchio!" cried the Fox, "give a little help to two poor, sick people!"

"Begone fakers!" answered the puppet. "You fooled me once, but you will never catch me again. If you are poor, you deserve it! Stolen money never brings any good." And thus saying, Pinocchio and Geppetto went their way in peace. Soon they came to a nice little straw hut with a roof of tiles and bricks. Pinocchio turned the key and they went in. The father and son looked round and saw the Talking Cricket. "Oh my dear little Cricket," said Pinocchio, "drive me away if you like, but have pity on my poor papa!"

"I will have pity on both father and son," said the Cricket, "but I wish to remind you of the bad treatment I got from you. I want to teach you that in this world we should show kindness to everybody, if we wish it to be given to us in our hour of need."

"You are right, dear Cricket, you are right, and I will remember the lesson you have given me. But tell me, where can I find a glass of milk for my dear Papa?"

The Destiny of Villains

"Three fields from here there lives a man who keeps cows," said the Cricket. "Go to him and you will get the milk you need."

Pinocchio ran all the way to the man's house. The man offered him a glass full of milk if he would work the pumping machine, which serves to draw up the water to water the vegetables. "If you will draw up a hundred buckets of water, I will give you a glass of milk," he said. Pinocchio began to work right away. Never before had he been so tired.

"Up till now, the labor of turning the pumping machine was performed by my little donkey, but now the animal is dying," said the man.

"May I see him?" asked Pinocchio. He went to the stable and saw a beautiful little donkey stretched out on the straw, worn-out from hunger and overwork. "I am sure I know this little donkey," said Pinocchio. And bending over the animal, he said in donkey language, "Who are you?"

"I am ... Can ... dle ... wick," said the donkey. And closing his eyes he died.

"Oh poor Candlewick," said Pinocchio in a low voice, and taking a handful of straw, he dried a tear that was rolling down his face.

From that day, for more than five months, he continued to get up at daybreak every morning to go and turn the pumping machine to work for glasses of milk that were so important to his father in his bad state of health. He also learned to make hampers and baskets, so he could make an honest living.

By his hard work, Pinocchio earned enough money to make his Papa well again. He also saved enough money to

Candlewick Dies

buy himself a new coat. One day, he was on his way to the tailor to order the coat, when he saw the Fairy's maid. "Oh tell me quickly, my beautiful little Snail," cried Pinocchio, "Where is my Fairy? What is she doing? Has she forgiven me? Does she still remember me? Is she well?"

"The Fairy is ill," said the Snail, "and has no money."

"Take this money then. It was to buy me a coat, but give it to my Fairy." The Snail quickly rushed off with Pinocchio's gift.

That night, Pinocchio worked until midnight, weaving baskets so that he could support his Papa and his beloved Fairy. Then he fell asleep. He dreamed that the Fairy kissed him and said, "Well done, Pinocchio! To reward you for your good heart I will forgive you for all that is past. Boys who take care of their parents deserve praise and love. Try to do better in the future and you will be happy."

You can guess Pinocchio's surprise when he woke up to find that he was no longer a wooden puppet. He had become a real boy, like all other boys.

Pinocchio ran into the next room and found his father in a good mood, carving in his new shop. Pinocchio joyfully said, "How silly I was when I was a puppet, and how glad I am that I have become a well-behaved little boy!"

The Real Boy

ABOUT THE ILLUSTRATOR

Greg Hildebrandt was born in Detroit, Michigan in 1939. As a child, Greg and his twin brother, Tim, loved to read. Even more, they loved pictures. They spent hours looking at the works of many famous artists. As they grew up, the twins learned to draw and paint. They moved to New Jersey and began to paint children's books. In 1976, they won a gold medal for being the best illustrators in America. Later, they painted the world-famous poster for the first "Star Wars" movie.

In 1983, Greg began illustrating the classics. He uses real people to pose for each character. Many of his models are his friends and family. Some of the books he has illustrated are *Peter Pan, Davy and the Goblin*, and *The Wizard of Oz*.